POWER

THE RISE AND FALL OF A POLITICIAN

VISHNU JOSHI

To the climbers, the fallers, and the survivors.

This is their story...

Contents

Foreword

The corridors of power are a seductive labyrinth. They whisper promises of influence, prestige, and the ability to shape the destiny of a nation. Many succumb to their allure, driven by ambition, idealism, or a desperate need for significance.

But what happens when the music stops? When the cheers fade, and the spotlight shifts elsewhere? What remains when the trappings of power are stripped away, and the politician is left to confront the emptiness that follows?

This book delves into the hidden underbelly of political life. It explores the psychological and emotional toll of the climb, the exhilaration of victory, and the agonizing descent into obscurity. Through the lens of a fictional or real-life protagonist, we witness the human cost of ambition, the fragility of power, and the enduring struggle to find meaning and purpose beyond the confines of office.

"Power Brake" is a cautionary tale, a mirror reflecting the complexities of human nature. It is a reminder that even the most powerful among us are vulnerable to the whims of fortune, the fragility of the human ego, and the enduring search for meaning in a world that often feels devoid of it.

I invite you to embark on this journey into the heart of power, to witness its allure and its inevitable decay.

-Vishnu Joshi

Preface

This book is a journey into the heart of political life – the highs, the lows, and everything in between. We'll explore what it's really like to climb the ladder of power, the intoxicating rush of success, and the bitter taste of defeat.

We'll meet our protagonist, a politician whose life is a whirlwind of ambition, compromise, and unexpected twists. We'll witness their rise to prominence, the challenges they face, and the difficult choices they must make.

But this isn't just a story about success. It's also about the human cost of ambition. What happens when the spotlight fades? How does a politician cope with the loss of power, the erosion of their influence, and the search for meaning in a life that suddenly feels empty?

This book is for anyone who has ever wondered what it's like to live in the public eye, to wield power, and to ultimately confront the inevitable reality of decline. It's a story about the human condition, about the fragility of power, and the enduring search for meaning in a world that is constantly changing.

Acknowledgements

This book would not have been possible without the countless individuals who, in their own way, have shaped my understanding of politics and the human condition. From the seasoned politicians I've observed, to the everyday citizens whose lives are impacted by their decisions, to the scholars and journalists who have illuminated the complexities of power, I am deeply grateful for their contributions, both conscious and unconscious.

While I cannot name them explicitly, I want to express my sincere gratitude to those who have shared their insights and experiences with me, whether through formal interviews, informal conversations, or simply by living their lives openly and honestly.

Their stories, their struggles, and their triumphs have provided the inspiration and the raw material for this book. Though their names may not appear on this page, their presence is felt throughout.

About Author

Vishnu Joshi is a Delhi-born advocate with a passion for social change and a keen interest in writing. He practiced law in the Supreme Court of India and the Delhi High Court, where his expertise and dedication to social justice made a significant impact. Vishnu's upbringing in a loving Hindu family instilled in him a strong sense of compassion, which fuels his commitment to serving the less fortunate. He is a visionary leader dedicated to creating a better world through his advocacy and writing.

@thevishnujoshi

About Editor

Yaman Joshi is a seasoned legal professional and social justice advocate. With a strong foundation in law and a deep-rooted commitment to human rights, Yaman brings a unique perspective to the editorial process. His academic qualifications include a law degree and a master's degree in social work, enabling him to analyze complex legal and social issues with nuance and precision.

Beyond his academic pursuits, Yaman has extensive experience as an editor for various journals. His keen eye for detail, coupled with his ability to critically assess content, ensures that each publication meets the highest standards of quality and rigor.

Yaman's passion for social justice is evident in his work. He is dedicated to amplifying marginalized voices and promoting equality and fairness. As an editor, he strives to create a platform for diverse perspectives and to foster meaningful dialogue on important social issues.

@theyamanjoshi

Introduction

In the world's largest democracy, power flows like the mighty rivers that crisscross our nation—sometimes life-giving, sometimes destructive, but always transformative. From the panchayat to the parliament, from municipal corporations to state assemblies, the journey of political power shapes not just institutions but the very souls of those who wield it.

This book peels back the layers of Indian democracy to examine how power transforms ordinary citizens into political figures and how that same power often leads to their eventual downfall. Through careful observation of patterns repeated across decades of democratic governance in India, we uncover universal truths about power's seductive nature and its corrupting influence.

CHAPTER ONE

THE BIRTH OF A POLITICIAN

In the dusty towns and bustling cities of India, political careers begin in three distinct ways, each leaving an indelible mark on those who choose to walk these paths.

The Family Legacy

In our political landscape, certain surnames carry the weight of generations. From national parties to regional powerhouses, political families have become institutions unto themselves. Children in these families don't just inherit assets; they inherit networks built over decades, loyalties cultivated through generations, and an intimate understanding of power's machinery.

Consider the scene at a typical political family's home during election season. The compound buzzes with activity from dawn to dusk. Party workers who served the candidate's father or grandfather now pledge allegiance to the next generation. Old photographs adorn the walls—grainy black and white images showing family patriarchs with freedom fighters, colored prints of more recent generations with prime ministers and presidents. Each image tells a story of accumulated influence, of doors that open more easily for some than others.

These political heirs often start young. They attend party meetings while still in school, learn to recognize important faces before they learn algebra, and understand power dynamics before they understand physics. Their education happens not just in classrooms but in drawing rooms where political strategies are crafted, at rally grounds where crowds are swayed, and in party offices where alliances are forged and broken.

Yet this inherited advantage comes with its own challenges. Every achievement is measured against their family's legacy. Every failure is magnified by the weight of their surname. The public eye scrutinizes them more closely, looking for signs of both greatness and weakness. Local media tracks their every move, comparing them constantly to their predecessors.

The Wealthy Entrant

The second path to power runs through the corridors of wealth. Successful industrialists, real estate magnates, and business leaders increasingly view political office as a natural extension of their influence. They bring substantial resources to the political arena—not just financial capital but organizational skills honed in the corporate world.

Their entry into politics often begins with local influence. Perhaps they've been supplying vehicles for party rallies, funding local festivals, or contributing to community initiatives. Gradually, they build a base of beneficiaries—people who have received help with medical bills, education expenses, or employment opportunities. This network of obligation and gratitude becomes the foundation for their political aspirations.

Their campaigns are well-oiled machines. Offices equipped with the latest technology, professional teams handling social media, strategists crafting messages, and extensive ground operations all backed by seemingly unlimited resources. They approach politics like a business venture—with detailed planning, clear targets, and efficient execution.

However, these wealthy aspirants often struggle to connect with ordinary voters. The air-conditioned offices and corporate efficiency can create distance from the very people whose support they seek. Their business success, while impressive, doesn't automatically translate into political acumen. The skills needed to manage employees differ greatly from those required to serve constituents.

The Grassroots Leader

The third path emerges from the ground up—through years of social work, community service, or activism. These are individuals who have spent years working directly with people, understanding their struggles firsthand, and fighting for their rights. Their political journey often begins in local movements—perhaps agitating for better water supply in their area, organizing farmers against land acquisition, or leading education initiatives for underprivileged children.

Their strength lies in their authentic connection with people. Years of working at the grassroots level give them an understanding that no amount of political training can provide. They know which streets flood during monsoons, which government offices are most corrupt, which schools lack teachers. Their support base is built on trust earned through consistent work rather than inherited influence or financial power.

These grassroots leaders often face significant challenges when entering formal politics. Their idealism confronts the harsh realities of campaign finance. Their genuine connection with communities must compete against well-funded political machines. Their straightforward approach to problems sometimes appears naive in the complex world of political maneuvering.

THE HONEY TRAP

The transformation begins subtly. A newly elected representative steps into their office for the first time, and the intoxicating symphony of power starts to play. It's a melody composed of small privileges that gradually accumulate into a crescendo of entitlement.

The Security Blanket

In India, political power comes wrapped in a security blanket—quite literally. The moment an individual assumes office, especially at the state or national level, they are enveloped in layers of protection that fundamentally alter their relationship with the world around them.

The morning after taking the oath, the new politician wakes up to find police personnel stationed outside their home. Black cats and commandos replace the local chowkidar. The transformation from ordinary citizen to "VIP" happens overnight. Where once they *walked freely through their constituency, now every movement is preceded by security checks and followed by armed escorts.*

This security apparatus, while necessary in many cases, creates an invisible barrier between the politician and the public. The same people who could once approach them directly at the local tea stall must now navigate through layers of security personnel. The immediate feedback loop of public interaction is replaced by filtered information passed through multiple intermediaries.

The Privileges of Office

The changes extend far beyond security. Government bungalows in prime locations, official vehicles with red beacons, staff at their beck and call—these trappings of power quickly become the new normal. The politician who once waited in queues now sees them part automatically. The person who struggled for appointments now makes others wait.

Consider the typical day of a minister in any Indian state. The morning begins with a stream of visitors waiting in their official residence's anteroom. Party workers who once treated them as equals now touch their feet, seeking blessings. Bureaucrats who might have ignored their phone calls now stand at attention in their presence. Business leaders who wouldn't give them the time of day now seek their "valuable guidance" on various matters.

Their words, once lost in the crowd, now make headlines. Local newspapers that ignored their press releases now analyze their every statement. Television channels that wouldn't give them five minutes now dedicate hour-long debates to their comments. Their ego, naturally, begins to inflate.

The Isolation of Power

Perhaps the most insidious effect of this transformation is the gradual isolation from reality. The politician who once traveled by local buses now moves in a convoy. The leader who understood the price of vegetables from weekly market visits now receives sanitized reports about inflation. The representative who once sat with constituents now views them through the tinted windows of their official vehicle.

This isolation is further reinforced by the emergence of a new ecosystem around them. A coterie of sycophants quickly forms, each member competing to please the newly powerful. These courtiers filter information, manipulate perceptions, and create an alternate reality where the politician is always right, always popular, always in control.

The feedback mechanisms that once kept them grounded start to break down. Criticism is filtered out by overzealous supporters. Bad news is sugar-coated by bureaucrats fearing transfers. The natural connection with ground reality, once their strength, begins to weaken.

The Financial Temptation

In a country where politics and money have a complex relationship, the financial aspects of power present their own honey trap. The politician's signature suddenly carries monetary weight. Files move or stall based on their words. Contracts are awarded or canceled at their behest. The power to affect financial decisions brings with it unprecedented temptations.

It begins innocently enough—perhaps with "well-wishers" paying for party functions or "supporters" sponsoring community events. Gradually, the lines between personal, political, and public finances begin to blur. The modest lifestyle that once connected them with voters starts to transform. Foreign trips, luxury cars, and lavish parties become the new normal.

The Erosion of Values

The most dangerous aspect of this honey trap is how it erodes the very values that might have led someone into public service. The fiery speeches against corruption give way to pragmatic acceptance of "how things work." The promises of transparency fade as the comfort of opacity sets in. The commitment to public service gradually transforms into a determination to retain power at any cost.

Consider how decisions are made in this new reality. The same politician who once organized protests against development projects affecting the poor might now clear similar projects with a single signature. The leader who demanded accountability in opposition now bristles at questions about their own actions. The representative who championed transparency now operates through layers of bureaucratic obscurity.

CHAPTER THREE

THE GREAT INDIAN ELECTION

In the world's largest democracy, elections are not merely political events—they are grand festivals of democracy that transform the nation every few years. From the Himalayan heights to coastal villages, from urban metropolises to tribal hamlets, the election machinery moves with precision, determination, and sometimes barely controlled chaos.

The Pre-Election Drama

Long before the Election Commission announces dates, the political climate begins to shift. Party offices that usually wear a deserted look suddenly buzz with activity. Old-timers who remember voter patterns from decades past become prized consultants. Young, tech-savvy workers armed with smartphones and social media expertise join the fray. The chess game of candidate selection begins.

This period reveals the first signs of power's corrupting influence. Ministers who haven't visited their constituencies in years suddenly become hyperactive. Development projects long gathering dust are hastily inaugurated. Promises dormant since the last election are hurriedly revived. The machinery of government strains under the sudden urgency to show "progress."

The Ticket Distribution Drama

Perhaps nowhere is the addiction to power more visible than during ticket distribution. Political parties become besieged fortresses, with aspirants camping outside party offices for days. The scenes inside these offices tell their own story of power's allure. Senior leaders who once preached party discipline now threaten to rebel if denied tickets. Wealthy aspirants offer to "fund the entire campaign." Local strongmen flex their "vote bank" muscles.

The political marketplace reaches its peak during this period. Party-hopping becomes an art form. Politicians who spent years criticizing rival parties suddenly discover their "inner calling" to join them. Principles that were non-negotiable yesterday become flexible today. The only constant is the desperate desire to remain in the power game.

The Campaign Trail

Once candidates are finalized, India witnesses a spectacle unmatched in scale and color. The election campaign transforms into a multi-billion rupee industry. Political consultants charge fees that would make corporate CEOs blush. Advertising agencies craft messages that blend local dialects with savvy marketing. Social media war rooms operate 24/7, manufacturing trends and managing perceptions.

The psychology of campaigning reveals deeper truths about power. Ministers accustomed to traveling in luxury now endure dusty roadshows. Leaders who won't take calls from ordinary citizens now touch the feet of village elders. The powerful temporarily become supplicants, but their actions betray their true nature. Watch carefully how they treat their party workers, how they respond to difficult questions, how they react when cameras aren't rolling.

Money Power and Muscle Power

Behind the democratic facade, darker forces are at work. Election expenditure limits exist on paper, but reality tells a different story. Conservative estimates suggest candidates spend tens of times the official limit. The source of this money? That's a question better left unasked in Indian politics.

The deployment of these resources follows well-established patterns. Early morning voters find currency notes slipped under their doors. Wedding expenses of community leaders are mysteriously taken care of. Local clubs receive generous donations for "cultural programs." The election season brings its own economy, its own rules of engagement.

Muscle power, though less visible than before, hasn't disappeared—it's evolved. Direct violence has been replaced by subtle intimidation. Booth capturing has given way to vote bank management. Local strongmen now present themselves as "community leaders," but their fundamental role remains unchanged.

The Role of Bureaucracy

The election machinery itself presents a fascinating study of power dynamics. Civil servants who normally jump at a minister's commands suddenly find their spine. The Model Code of Conduct becomes a shield behind which bureaucrats deny political requests they've been fulfilling for years. The power equation temporarily shifts, though everyone knows it's temporary.

For many politicians, this period is their first taste of powerlessness in years. The official vehicle must be surrendered. The government bungalow can't be used for campaign meetings. The police escort is withdrawn. Watch how different politicians handle this temporary reduction in their power—it reveals much about their character.

The Media Circus

Media coverage during elections offers another window into power's influence. News channels hungry for content and advertising revenue become willing participants in the political theater. Studio debates generate more heat than light. Opinion polls become bargaining chips. Political analysts multiply overnight.

The smartest politicians understand this game well. They know which channels need TRP boosts, which anchors need exclusive interviews, which media houses need government advertising. The quid pro quo may not be explicit, but it's understood by all players.

Election Day Drama

The actual voting day brings its own revelations about power. Watch established politicians on polling day—their behavior is telling. Some maintain their VIP airs even in polling booths. Others put on an elaborate show of being "common citizens." The truly powerful often don't even bother to manage things personally—their well-oiled machinery runs on autopilot.

The most fascinating period is between voting and counting. Political leaders who publicly claim certain victory privately conduct desperate negotiations. Hotel rooms are booked in bulk for "resort politics." Horse-trading allegations fly thick and fast. The politics of power reaches its purest form in these uncertain hours.

CHAPTER FOUR

THE DANCE OF POWER

Victory in Indian politics marks not just the end of an election but the beginning of a profound transformation. The day after the results, everything changes—not just for the winner, but for everyone in their orbit. This metamorphosis offers perhaps the most revealing insights into power's true nature.

The Morning After

The transformation begins literally overnight. The politician who was accessible to all during campaigns suddenly becomes surrounded by layers of gatekeepers. Their personal phone number, freely distributed during the election season, now routes to assistants. The humble demeanor of the candidate transforms into the authoritative bearing of the elected representative.

Watch closely as the winner's residence transforms. Security personnel appear at the gates. Visitors who could walk in freely yesterday must now register their names. The modest chair from campaign days is replaced by an ornate seat befitting their new status. Even the tea served to visitors changes—from the roadside vendor's cutting chai to premium brands in bone china cups.

The Power Ecosystem

Within days, a new ecosystem forms around the victor. This inner circle typically includes:
• The Political Advisor: Often a seasoned operator who understands the wheels within wheels of power.
• The Personal Secretary: Gatekeeper supreme, wielding enormous derivative power.
• The Media Manager: Tasked with image building and damage control.
• The Resource Manager: Handling the delicate matter of finances, often operating in the shadows.
• The Community Coordinators: Maintaining links with various vote banks.
• The Local Strongmen: Providing muscle power when needed, usually kept at arm's length publicly.

This ecosystem serves as both a buffer and a barrier—protecting the politician from direct pressures while simultaneously isolating them from ground realities.
The Bureaucratic Ballet

Perhaps nowhere is the dance of power more evident than in the politician's interaction with the bureaucracy. Watch how officers who ignored their calls during elections now stand at attention in their presence. District officials who cited rule books to deny appointments now find creative solutions to accommodate their requests.

This relationship becomes a delicate ballet. The politician needs bureaucrats to implement their vision (or serve their interests). The bureaucrats need political support for postings and promotions. Both sides engage in an elaborate dance of mutual dependency, each trying to maintain leverage over the other.
The Intoxication of Authority

Power manifests in myriad ways, each more seductive than the last:
• The ability to make others wait (while arriving late themselves).
• The power to transfer officials with a single phone call.
• The authority to approve or stall projects worth crores.
• The capacity to influence police investigations.

• *The privilege of having their opinions become headlines.*
• *The ability to make or break the careers of subordinates.*

Each of these capabilities acts like a drop of slow poison, gradually eroding the connection with normal life. The politician who once prided themselves on being "one among the people" increasingly starts seeing themselves as above the common citizen.

The God Complex

This is where many politicians develop what can only be called a god complex. Signs include:
• Expecting people to touch their feet.
• Refusing to walk short distances (must be driven).
• Demanding special treatment everywhere.
• Using their position to bend rules.
• Expecting public events to begin only upon their arrival.
• Treating criticism as a personal insult.

This behavior stems not just from ego but from the constant reinforcement provided by sycophants. When everyone around you treats you like a deity, it becomes easy to start believing in your own infallibility.

The Erosion of Independence

Paradoxically, as official power increases, personal independence often decreases. The politician becomes increasingly dependent on their ecosystem:
• *Security personnel must accompany them everywhere.*
• *Assistants must handle all communications.*
• *Party workers must manage public interactions.*
• *Media managers must control their image.*
• *Resource managers must handle finances.*

This dependency creates a golden cage—comfortable but constraining. The politician's world shrinks even as their influence expands.

The Price of Power

The cost of maintaining power becomes increasingly evident:
• *Family life suffers as politics demands 24/7 attention.*
• *Old friendships fade as status differences create barriers.*
• *Genuine feedback becomes rare as sycophancy increases.*
• *Personal freedom diminishes under security protocols.*

• *The ability to enjoy simple pleasures is lost.*
• *Paranoia often sets in about potential rivals and threats.*

Yet few are willing to step away from power voluntarily. The intoxication is too strong, the addiction too deep.

CHAPTER FIVE

THE ILLUSION OF INVINCIBILITY

The swearing-in ceremony stands as a watershed moment in any politician's life. Under the glare of cameras and the watchful eyes of dignitaries, the oath of office marks not just a formal assumption of power but often the beginning of a psychological transformation. What unfolds in the days, months, and years that follow reveals how power can create an almost impenetrable bubble of perceived invincibility.

For many, the changes begin within hours of taking the oath. The modest office they once occupied transforms into a palatial chamber, its very architecture designed to intimidate visitors and reinforce authority. The worn furniture of campaign days gives way to leather-backed chairs and polished wooden desks. Even the air feels different, perfumed with the subtle scent of power that wafts through the corridors of government buildings.

The phone calls, once politely made and humbly received, now carry an unspoken weight of authority. A minister's request becomes a command, their suggestion an order. The same officials who might have ignored their calls during the campaign now scramble to answer on the first ring. Their signature, once a mere formality on party documents, now has the power to move millions, approve projects, and alter lives.

The transformation extends to their living spaces. Government bungalows, those coveted symbols of power in every state capital, become their new homes. These colonial-era structures, with their sprawling lawns and high ceilings, further separate them from the reality of ordinary citizens. The presence of security personnel, once a temporary arrangement during campaigns, becomes a permanent fixture. Armed guards stand at attention, their very presence creating a physical barrier between the powerful and the public.

The power of office amplifies ego in ways both subtle and profound. Every decision, no matter how minor, is treated with excessive importance. Party tickets, once a matter of democratic deliberation within the party, become personal fiefdoms. The power to decide candidacies turns into a tool for rewarding loyalty and punishing dissent. The voices that once offered honest feedback are gradually silenced, replaced by a chorus of agreement from sycophants.

Yet beneath this veneer of absolute power lies a more complex reality. Most politicians, even those holding ministerial positions, remain answerable to higher authorities within their party structure. The very individual who pulled strings to elevate them to power—often referred to as their "godfather" in political circles—continues to exercise control. Despite their newfound authority, they remain "chintu"—small fry in the larger scheme of things.

This paradox creates interesting dynamics. While wielding seemingly absolute power in their domain, they must constantly demonstrate loyalty to their political mentors. Every decision must be weighed not just for its merit but for its potential impact on their relationship with party higher-ups. Their independence, despite their official position, remains curtailed.

The public, however, remains largely unaware of these internal power dynamics. They see only the outward manifestations of authority—the cavalcade of vehicles, the deferential treatment by officials, the grandstanding at public functions. The crowds that gather outside their residences each morning grow larger and more sycophantic. During festivals and special occasions, the clamor for their attention reaches a fever pitch.

The trappings of power create their own momentum. Every public appearance becomes a carefully choreographed event. Their words, no matter how mundane, are treated as profound statements of policy. Local media hangs on their every utterance, turning routine comments into headlines. This constant attention and deference further feed their sense of invincibility.

The erosion of transparency often accompanies this growing god complex. Official documents that once meticulously detailed their assets seem to develop convenient gaps. The affidavits filed during elections become exercises in creative accounting. The same politician who once championed transparency now finds numerous reasons to avoid scrutiny of their personal wealth.

The distance between the politician and the people widens with each passing day in office. The same leader who once prided themselves on being accessible to all now becomes increasingly isolated behind layers of bureaucracy and protocol. This isolation isn't merely physical—it's psychological, creating a deepening disconnect from the very people they're meant to serve.

The manifestation of the god complex becomes increasingly evident in their daily routines. Meetings scheduled for 10 AM don't begin until noon, with dozens of people waiting patiently for hours. This ability to make others wait—from business leaders to bureaucrats—becomes a subtle demonstration of power. Time itself becomes a tool to reinforce their perceived importance.

Their travel arrangements reflect this growing sense of invincibility. Even for short distances within the city, a convoy of vehicles becomes necessary. The route must be cleared, traffic stopped, and security personnel positioned at every junction. What might have been a simple fifteen-minute journey transforms into an elaborate operation, with pilot vehicles, ambulances, and security details all playing their assigned roles.

The power bubble extends to their family members, who begin to share in this sense of invincibility. Children who once traveled by public transport now expect government vehicles for their personal use. Relatives who maintained low profiles suddenly become influential power brokers. The family home, once open to constituents, transforms into a fortress with restricted access.

Protocol becomes a shield behind which they retreat from reality. Official functions must follow elaborate ceremonies—the traditional welcome, the lighting of lamps, the presentation of bouquets. Each ritual reinforces their elevated status, creating an ever-thickening layer of separation from ordinary life. The simple act of meeting people transforms into a durbar, where supplicants must approach with appropriate deference and respect.

The media's role in this transformation cannot be understated. Local newspapers that once criticized their actions now print flattering profiles. Television channels that questioned their policies now broadcast lengthy interviews where tough questions are conspicuously absent. This shift in media treatment further reinforces their sense of invulnerability. Press conferences become rare, replaced by carefully managed interactions where difficult questions are screened out.

Their official residence becomes a power center in itself. The welcome area fills with people seeking favors—contractors hoping for projects, officials requesting transfers, party workers needing recommendations. Each supplicant's presence reinforces their sense of importance. The power to grant or deny requests becomes intoxicating, leading to increasingly arbitrary decision-making.

The corruption of power manifests most clearly in their changing lifestyle. Despite no visible increase in their official income, their standard of living rises dramatically. Foreign trips become frequent, designer clothes replace traditional attire, and luxury vehicles appear in their convoy. Yet questions about these *changes are dismissed or ignored, protected by their perceived untouchability.*

Their speech patterns and body language undergo subtle but significant changes. The humble tone of the candidate gives way to the authoritative voice of power. Simple requests become commands, suggestions turn into orders. Even their posture changes—the forward lean of attention replaced by the backward tilt of authority. Every gesture is calculated to reinforce their elevated status.

The annual festival season particularly highlights this transformation. Their residence becomes a center of activity, with hundreds visiting to offer greetings and seek blessings. The very act of receiving these visitors from an elevated position, often seated on an ornate chair while others stand, reinforces their god-like status. The offerings they receive—from expensive gifts to elaborate bouquets—further feed their sense of importance.

Office dynamics reflect their growing detachment from reality. Civil servants who once offered honest advice learn to tell them what they want to hear. Files that contain unpleasant truths are quietly buried under paperwork. The entire administrative machinery gradually adapts to protect their illusions rather than present facts.

This bubble of invincibility affects their decision-making abilities. Policy decisions are made not based on public need but on personal convenience or political advantage. Development projects are approved not for their merit but for their ability to enhance the leader's image. The distinction between public good and personal benefit becomes increasingly blurred.

Their security detail, originally meant for protection, becomes another tool of power projection. The size of their convoy, the number of guards, the elaborate security protocols—all become measures of their importance. The ability to disrupt normal life—stopping traffic, clearing roads, cordoning off areas—becomes a daily demonstration of their authority.

Yet beneath this edifice of invincibility, cracks begin to appear. Loyal party workers who remember their early days start maintaining their distance. Old friends who could once speak freely now hesitate to offer honest opinions. The very isolation that makes them feel powerful also makes them vulnerable, cutting them off from ground realities and crucial feedback.

The transformation is perhaps most evident during election seasons. The same leader who once walked from door to door now considers it beneath their dignity to directly seek votes. Campaign speeches become pronouncements from high pedestals rather than conversations with voters. The connection with common citizens, once their strength, becomes their biggest weakness.

This illusion of invincibility, built over years of power and privilege, creates a dangerous blindness to changing political winds. They fail to notice the growing public resentment, the whispered criticisms, the declining attendance at their functions. Protected by layers of sycophants and yes-men, they remain convinced of their unchangeable position until the moment of their eventual fall.

The tragedy of this transformation lies in its predictability. History offers countless examples of leaders who succumbed to the same illusion, yet each new generation of politicians convinces itself that they are different, that their power is more secure, their position more stable. The god complex, once established, resists all attempts at correction until reality finally breaks through.

CHAPTER SIX

THE VELVET CAGE

The Minister's life had become a symphony of sirens. Not the wailing sirens of an emergency, but the soft, seductive siren song of power. It began subtly, almost imperceptibly. The initial thrill of authority, the heady rush of making decisions that impacted millions, had given way to a more insidious addiction—the addiction to the trappings of power, to the constant validation, to the feeling of being above the fray.

The Office Sanctuary

The office, once a place of work, had transformed into a sanctuary of power. The white towel draped over the armrest of his chair became more than just fabric—it was a symbol of his elevated status. He savored the ritual of it, the cool linen against his skin, a small indulgence that whispered of privilege. The constant stream of visitors, each vying for his attention, each eager to please, further inflated his ego. He reveled in the deference, the hushed tones, the respectful nods.

Every morning brought its own ceremony of power. The opening of doors, the salutes from the guards, the orchestrated symphony of arrival—these were the daily rituals that reinforced his sense of importance. Even the arrangement of his office spoke of authority—the carefully positioned chair that placed him slightly higher than visitors, the strategic placement of religious symbols and family photographs, the expensive pen set that was more for show than use.

The Travel Ritual

Travel had become an exercise in privilege. He had grown accustomed to the red-carpet treatment at airports, the expedited security checks, the hushed whispers of admiration. He preferred to arrive late at the airport, savoring the privilege of last-minute boarding, a small act of defiance against the constraints of ordinary travel. The 1A seat, a symbol of his elevated status, became his throne, a place where he could survey the world below, a world of lesser mortals.

Even domestic travel had its own protocol. The convoy of vehicles, the pilot cars, the security detail—all carefully choreographed to demonstrate his importance. Roads would be cleared, traffic stopped, ordinary citizens made to wait while his cavalcade passed. The power to disrupt normal life had become a daily affirmation of his authority.

The Social Performance

His social life had become a carefully choreographed performance. Every public appearance, every social gathering, was an opportunity to project an image of power and influence. His wardrobe was meticulously curated, each outfit a statement of wealth and status. Even his morning walks were conducted with a sense of theater, a conscious awareness that the media might be watching, that every step was being scrutinized.

The selection of events to attend had become a strategic exercise. Each appearance was weighed for its political value, its potential for image enhancement. Private functions were evaluated based on the host's importance, the guest list, the media coverage expected. Even religious ceremonies became opportunities for power projection, with special arrangements and preferential treatment reinforcing his VIP status.

The Family Distance

The demands of his position had also distanced him from his family and friends. The constant pressure to maintain his public image, the relentless demands of his schedule, had left little room for personal relationships. His family, once a source of comfort and support, now felt like distant observers in his life of power. Dinner conversations revolved around political strategies rather than personal connections. Children grew up seeing more of their father in newspapers than at home.
His friends, once close confidantes, had become mere acquaintances, their conversations dominated by polite inquiries about his political career. The easy laughter of old friendships had been replaced by careful words and measured responses. Even casual meet-ups required security clearances and protocol considerations, making spontaneous interactions impossible.

The Taste of Luxury

He had grown accustomed to the finer things in life—the exquisite cuisine, the luxurious accommodations, the exclusive social circles. The taste of power, the intoxicating blend of privilege and adulation, had corrupted his palate. Simple pleasures no longer satisfied; everything had to be exceptional, exclusive, extraordinary. A regular cup of tea had been replaced by premium blends served in fine bone china. Local restaurants were forgotten in favor of five-star hotels where chefs prepared special meals.

The Burden of Expectation

The weight of expectation, the constant scrutiny, the relentless pressure to perform—it all took its toll. He experienced moments of doubt, fleeting glimpses of the life he had left behind. Late at night, lying awake in his luxurious government bungalow, he would think of his childhood, of his dreams, of the man he had once hoped to become. But these thoughts were fleeting, quickly dismissed as mere distractions from the importance of his position.

Every public appearance required careful preparation. His clothes needed to reflect his status while appearing appropriately humble. His words had to demonstrate authority while showing a connection with common people. Even his gestures were scrutinized—a namaste too deep might show weakness, while one too shallow could suggest arrogance.

The Security Cocoon

Security personnel had become his constant companions, their presence both protecting and isolating him. They accompanied him everywhere—morning walks, family functions, temple visits. Their earpieces, dark glasses, and alert postures created an invisible barrier between him and the world. What began as protection had evolved into a wall, separating him from genuine human contact. The protocol extended to his family as well. His children couldn't simply go to a movie or a restaurant without security arrangements. His wife's shopping trips required advance planning and security coordination. Even family weddings became high-security events, with guests passing through metal detectors and security checks.

The Loss of Privacy

Privacy had become a distant memory. Every move, every meeting, every phone call was logged and monitored. Security cameras watched his official residence, pilot cars tracked his movements, and intelligence officials monitored his interactions. The very machinery meant to protect him had become his surveiller, creating a gilded cage where every action was observed and recorded.

Even his personal moments were not truly personal. Family celebrations became photo opportunities, private conversations risked becoming public statements, and casual remarks could turn into headlines. The constant awareness of being watched had changed his behavior, making him more guarded, more calculated, less spontaneous.

The Addiction to Deference

Perhaps the most insidious aspect of the velvet cage was the addiction to deference. He had grown used to people standing when he entered a room, to files moving faster on his word, to officials jumping to attention at his arrival. This constant reinforcement of his importance had become necessary for his emotional well-being.

The rare occasions when he didn't receive this deference felt like personal affronts.
His definition of normal had shifted dramatically. A slight delay in his convoy sparked irritation. A junior officer's failure to recognize him immediately caused annoyance. The absence of proper protocol at any function became a matter of serious concern. The trappings of power had become essential to his sense of self.

The Time Trap

Time itself behaved differently in his world. His time had become more valuable than others', leading to a strange relationship with punctuality.

While others were expected to arrive early and wait, he could arrive at his convenience. Meetings scheduled for morning might begin in the afternoon, with dozens of people waiting patiently. This power over others' time had become another addiction, another bar in his velvet cage.

The Erosion of Reality

He had become a prisoner of his own creation, trapped in a gilded cage of his own making. The sirens of power, once a seductive melody, had now become a haunting lullaby, lulling him into a false sense of security, blinding him to the dangers that lurked beneath the surface. The very comfort of his position had become his greatest vulnerability.

The velvet cage had done its work perfectly—it had separated him from reality while making the separation feel like elevation. His world had become more comfortable but less real, more luxurious but less free. The soft chains of privilege bound him as surely as iron shackles, but their velvet coating made them feel like ornaments rather than restraints.

CHAPTER SEVEN

THE INCUMBENCY: PEOPLE VS. PALACE

The velvet cage had become a prison. The Minister, once a champion of the people, had become a dictator, his grip on power tightening with each passing day. The initial euphoria of victory had long since faded, replaced by a cold, calculating ambition. The people, who had once showered him with affection, now felt like distant echoes, their voices muffled by the roar of his own ambition.

The Transformation of Authority

The illusion of invincibility, once a source of strength, had now become a dangerous delusion. Where once he saw himself as a servant of the people, he now viewed himself as their master.

The transformation was complete—from representative to ruler, from public servant to autocrat. Every trapping of power reinforced this shift, from the armed guards at his gate to the officials who trembled in his presence.

The public meetings, once vibrant forums for democratic dialogue, had devolved into carefully orchestrated shows of power. Gone were the days of open discussion and genuine feedback. Instead, party workers carefully selected attendees, screened questions, and managed optics. The Minister would arrive hours late, deliver a lengthy monologue, and depart without taking questions, leaving behind a wake of frustration and resentment.

The Erosion of Democracy

The systematic weakening of democratic processes happened gradually but relentlessly. Opposition voices were marginalized through various tactics—denial of permits for rallies, selective enforcement of regulations, targeted investigations. The local media, once vigorous in its criticism, found itself under pressure through control of government advertising and subtle intimidation.

Even within his own party, dissent was no longer tolerated. Party meetings became exercises in sycophancy, with members competing to praise his leadership rather than discuss real issues. Those who dared to question decisions found themselves sidelined, their political careers effectively ended. The party structure, meant to provide checks and balances, had become a mere rubber stamp for his decisions.

The Fear Factor

Fear, not of the people but of their response, now consumed him. He began avoiding unscripted public appearances, preferring the safety of controlled environments. His movements became increasingly restricted, his public interactions more choreographed. The same streets he once walked freely now had to be sanitized before his convoy could pass.

The security apparatus around him grew exponentially, not just in response to actual threats but as a buffer against public contact. What began as reasonable protection had morphed into an impenetrable barrier between him and his constituents. The distance between the palace and the people grew wider with each passing day.

The Governance Vacuum

The past year had been particularly revealing. While inflation soared and unemployment rose, he spent his time jet-setting abroad, attending conferences and ceremonies far from the problems of his constituency. The disconnect between his lifestyle and the struggles of ordinary citizens became increasingly apparent. Development projects stalled, public services deteriorated, but the Minister remained insulated in his bubble of power.

His office, once bustling with activity and purpose, had become a fortress of bureaucratic inertia. Files moved slowly, decisions were delayed, and public grievances piled up unaddressed. The energy and enthusiasm that marked his early days in office had been replaced by a combination of arrogance and apathy.

The Public Response

The people, once his devoted supporters, watched this transformation with growing alarm. The promises of development remained unfulfilled, while the visible signs of his personal prosperity multiplied. New vehicles appeared in his convoy, foreign trips became more frequent, and his children were sent to study abroad. Yet questions about these changes were met with hostility and threats.

At public functions, the crowds grew thinner, though official photographs always showed packed venues. The spontaneous affection of earlier years was replaced by paid applause and orchestrated celebrations. Even festival celebrations, once occasions for genuine public connection, became exclusive events with restricted access and heavy security.

The Administrative Breakdown

The bureaucracy, meant to serve as the bridge between government and people, had become a wall instead. Officials, taking cues from their political master, grew increasingly unresponsive to public needs. Corruption, once checked by political oversight, flourished in the absence of accountability. The entire administrative machinery seemed to exist solely to serve the Minister's interests rather than public welfare.

The Media Manipulation

The Minister's relationship with the media underwent a dramatic transformation. Independent journalists found themselves excluded from briefings, their questions ignored, their access restricted. Instead, a select group of friendly media houses received exclusive interviews, where pre-approved questions led to rehearsed responses. Critical coverage was denounced as "fake news" or "motivated journalism."

Social media teams worked around the clock to project an image of successful governance. Positive comments were amplified, criticism was systematically removed, and paid campaigns created an illusion of popular support. Real public sentiment, however, found expression in private conversations and anonymous online forums, where frustration and disappointment grew unchecked.

The Economic Impact

The economic consequences of this disconnect became increasingly apparent. Local businesses, once flourishing under stable governance, struggled with arbitrary decisions and unclear policies. Government contracts went to a select group of favored contractors, while small entrepreneurs faced mounting bureaucratic hurdles. The economy of the constituency began to reflect the same inequality that characterized its governance—a small group prospering while the majority struggled.

Development projects, when implemented, seemed designed more for visibility than utility. Grand schemes were announced with much fanfare but executed poorly or left incomplete. Infrastructure development focused on areas frequented by VIPs while neglecting crucial public needs. The gap between official claims of progress and ground reality widened with each passing day.

The Feedback Failure

The system of public feedback, once a crucial part of democratic governance, had completely broken down. Letters from citizens went unanswered, complaints remained unaddressed, and grievance cells existed only on paper. The Minister's office, once accessible to common people, now required multiple appointments and clearances just for a brief meeting.

Even party workers, traditionally the eyes and ears of political leadership, hesitated to convey negative feedback. Those who dared to report public discontent found themselves sidelined or ignored. The resulting information vacuum left the Minister completely disconnected from growing public dissatisfaction.

The Security State

The security apparatus had grown into a symbol of separation between ruler and ruled. Roads were blocked for his convoy, public spaces were cleared for his visits, and ordinary citizens faced harassment in the name of VIP security. What began as necessary protection had become a tool of public intimidation.

Government buildings, meant to serve the public, transformed into fortresses. Security checks became more rigorous, access more restricted, and the common citizen more alienated. The physical barriers reflected a deeper psychological wall between the administration and the people it was meant to serve.

The Personal Bubble

The Minister's personal life had become completely detached from ordinary reality. His children studied in foreign universities, his family shopped abroad, and his social circle comprised only the elite. The understanding of common issues—the price of vegetables, the state of public transport, the quality of government schools—was completely lost.

His daily routine reflected this disconnect. Mornings began with sycophantic party workers bringing selective news reports. Afternoons were spent in air-conditioned offices far removed from the summer heat that his constituents endured. Evenings featured exclusive gatherings where mutual admiration replaced genuine discussion of public issues.

The Power Addiction

The addiction to power manifested in increasingly arbitrary behavior. Decisions were made on whims rather than merit. Officials were transferred based on personal loyalty rather than performance. Development funds were allocated to showcase projects rather than addressing basic needs. The intoxication of authority had completely overshadowed the responsibility of public service.

This arbitrariness extended to his personal conduct. Public functions started hours late because he couldn't be bothered with punctuality. Government resources were used for personal convenience without any sense of impropriety. The line between public duty and personal privilege had completely disappeared.

The Democratic Deficit

The erosion of democratic values became most evident in his attitude toward the opposition. Political opponents faced not just political resistance but administrative harassment. Their public meetings were denied permission, their supporters faced subtle threats, and their legitimate protests were suppressed using state machinery.

Even within democratic institutions, his influence worked to undermine checks and balances. Local bodies were stripped of autonomy, oversight committees were packed with loyalists, and independent voices were systematically silenced. The democracy he was sworn to protect had become a casualty of his authoritarian tendencies.

The Public Awakening

However, beneath the surface of controlled media narratives and manipulated public opinion, a change was brewing. People began sharing their experiences on social media, bypassing traditional information controls. Local groups started documenting unfulfilled promises and failed projects. The very tools of modern communication that he used for propaganda became instruments of public awakening.

Community organizations, despite facing obstacles, started asserting their rights. RTI activists began questioning financial decisions. Youth groups started comparing his promises with actual delivery. The public, though silent, was neither blind nor forgetful.

The Signs of Decline

The signs of political decline were visible to everyone except those within the power bubble. Attendance at public functions had to be bolstered with paid crowds. Genuine public enthusiasm had been replaced by orchestrated celebrations. The spontaneous gatherings that once marked his public appearances had given way to carefully managed photo opportunities.

Yet, surrounded by sycophants and cut off from reality, he remained convinced of his invincibility. The very isolation that made him vulnerable had also blinded him to his vulnerability. The palace had completely lost touch with the people, setting the stage for an inevitable fall.

CHAPTER EIGHT

THE DANCE OF DEMOCRACY

Ten years. A decade of power had slipped through his fingers like grains of sand, leaving behind nothing but the hollow echo of unfulfilled promises. The election schedule on the Minister's desk now seemed like a death warrant for his political career. The upcoming elections loomed not as an opportunity to reconnect with voters, but as a final reckoning for years of disconnect and neglect.

The Weight of Time

The past decade had been a study in opportunities squandered and responsibilities ignored. While common citizens struggled with rising prices and unemployment, he had focused on expanding his personal empire. His assets had multiplied mysteriously—new properties sprouted up like mushrooms after rain, his bank accounts swelled with unexplained deposits, and his lifestyle grew *increasingly lavish. All built on the foundation of public trust, though he would never admit it openly.*

The stark reality of his situation hit him hard as he reviewed his constituency's development records. The papers before him told a story of systematic neglect. There were no significant achievements to showcase, no transformative projects to point to with pride. The roads he had promised remained unpaved, the hospitals understaffed, the schools in disrepair. His speeches, once filled with grand visions and bold promises, now rang hollow even in his own ears.

The Electoral Challenge

The festival of democracy was once again in full swing across the nation, but this time it felt different. Campaign vehicles wound their way through dusty streets, loudspeakers blared political slogans, and colorful posters plastered every available surface. Yet, unlike previous elections, where he had approached campaigns with supreme confidence, this time an unfamiliar sensation gripped him—fear.

His traditional constituency, once a stronghold, now seemed like hostile territory. Reports from party workers were alarming—the people were angry, disillusioned, and eager for change.

The very voters who had once worshipped him as their savior now spoke of betrayal and neglect. The whispers of dissent had grown into a roar that even his most loyal supporters couldn't ignore.

The Search for Safety

In desperate meetings with his advisors, he pored over electoral maps and polling data, searching for a safe seat—any seat where victory seemed assured. The idea of losing was unthinkable.

The very thought of life without power, without the trappings of office that had become as essential as breathing, filled him with dread. He had forgotten how to live as an ordinary citizen; the decade of VIP treatment had erased all memory of a simpler life.

The suggestion of fighting from two seats emerged during one late-night strategy session, his voice betraying barely concealed panic. It was a common tactic among politicians uncertain of victory, a way to hedge their bets. His advisors nodded dutifully, though their eyes held doubt. They knew as well as he did that such a move would be seen as a sign of weakness, an admission of fear.

The Financial Reality

The election deposit—once a trivial matter—now weighed heavily on his mind. The thought of losing it, of facing not just defeat but humiliation, was unbearable. He had heard whispers of other politicians who had lost everything, their security deposits forfeit, their political careers ended in disgrace. These stories, once distant cautionary tales, now felt uncomfortably personal.

His days became an endless cycle of meetings with power brokers and local leaders, attempting to shore up support through promises and negotiations. Money flowed freely, though carefully concealed behind layers of middlemen and front organizations. The Election Commission's guidelines were treated as mere inconveniences to be circumvented, not rules to be followed.

The Campaign Challenge

The political landscape had shifted beneath his feet while he remained ensconced in his bubble of power. The voters, once easily swayed by grand promises and theatrical gestures, had become more discerning, more demanding of actual results. They asked uncomfortable questions about his wealth, about the disparity between his declared assets and his lavish lifestyle.

His campaign speeches, once delivered with confidence and flair, now felt forced and defensive. Every public meeting became an exercise in explanation—why roads weren't built, why jobs weren't created, why promises weren't kept. The connection with the audience, once natural and effortless, had been lost in years of isolation and indifference.

The Digital Battlefield

Social media, that double-edged sword of modern politics, had become a battlefield he couldn't control. Videos of his old promises circulated widely, juxtaposed with the reality of unfulfilled development goals. Memes mocked his transformation from a supposed servant of the people to a distant, unapproachable figure surrounded by security and sycophants.

His social media team worked overtime trying to counter negative narratives, but their efforts felt increasingly futile. The carefully crafted posts and professionally shot videos couldn't mask the underlying disconnect. Every attempted explanation seemed to dig a deeper hole, every clarification raised more questions.

The Personal Cost

In quiet moments, when the mask of confidence slipped, he confronted the emptiness of his legacy. Ten years in power, and what did he have to show for it? Personal wealth, yes, but at what cost? The respect of the people, once freely given, had been squandered. The trust they had placed in him had been betrayed.

His personal life bore the scars of his choices. Family relationships had withered under the harsh light of public scrutiny and his own neglect. Friends from his early days, those who had known him before power changed him, had gradually drifted away, unable to recognize the person he had become. Even his closest advisors, he suspected, stayed more out of self-interest than loyalty.

The Desperate Measures

As the election dates drew closer, his desperation grew more evident. He began making outlandish promises—free electricity, loan waivers, guaranteed jobs—knowing full well they were impossible to fulfill. He attacked his opponents with increasing viciousness, hoping to divert attention from his own failures. The refined facade of statesmanship crumbled, revealing the frightened politician beneath.

The safe seat he sought remained elusive. Each potential constituency came with its own risks, its own complications. The party high command, once solidly behind him, now seemed to be hedging their bets, preparing for all possibilities. The sycophants who had once crowded his anteroom began to thin out, sensing perhaps that the wind was changing direction.

The Moment of Truth

In his more honest moments, he acknowledged that this crisis was entirely of his own making. He had had opportunities—countless opportunities—to make a real difference, to leave a lasting legacy of positive change. Instead, he had chosen personal gain over public service, power over responsibility, luxury over duty.

The irony wasn't lost on him—that the very power he had so desperately clung to might now slip from his grasp precisely because of how he had wielded it. The lifestyle he had grown accustomed to, the privileges he took for granted, the authority he had abused—all of it stood on the brink of disappearing.

The Final Days

As election day approached, the facade of confidence became harder to maintain. Every opinion poll brought bad news, every internal survey showed declining support. The crowds at his rallies, despite being paid to attend, seemed listless and unresponsive. The energy that had characterized his earlier campaigns was conspicuously absent.

His speeches became increasingly disconnected from reality, promising solutions to problems he had ignored for years. The more he spoke, the less people seemed to listen. The disconnect between his words and his actions over the past decade was too stark to ignore.

The Legacy Question

The prospect of defeat forced him to confront questions about his legacy. What would he be remembered for? The promises he broke? The wealth he accumulated? The trust he betrayed? The development he neglected? These thoughts haunted his campaign travels, making each speech more difficult than the last.

His attempts to showcase achievements turned into embarrassments as locals pointed out incomplete projects and unfulfilled promises. Every inauguration stone he had laid stood as a monument to promises broken, every foundation ceremony a reminder of dreams unfulfilled.

The Final Realization

As he sat in his office, watching the sun set over the city he had failed to serve, the Minister confronted the possibility that this might be one of his last evenings in power. The thought filled him with a terror he had never known before. What awaited him on the other side of defeat? How would he face a world where doors didn't automatically open, where crowds didn't part, where his word wasn't law?

The coming elections would answer these questions, one way or another. But for now, he remained trapped in his desperate dance, searching for a way to maintain his grip on power, even as it slipped inexorably through his fingers. The festival of democracy, once his triumph, had become his trial, and the verdict lay in the hands of the very people he had forgotten to serve.

CHAPTER NINE

THE FALL

The counting center hummed with tension on that fateful morning. Electronic Voting Machines beeped methodically, each sound echoing through the hall like a hammer blow to the Minister's rapidly crumbling world. The first round of counting had barely finished, and already his worst nightmares were materializing before his eyes.

The Morning of Reckoning

The day began early, though sleep had been elusive the night before. The Minister's residence, usually bustling with activity, felt eerily quiet. Even the permanent fixtures of his political life—the perpetually present party workers, the hovering assistants, the eager reporters—seemed subdued. The morning newspapers lay untouched; their headlines already felt irrelevant against the weight of the coming hours.

Security personnel, who had been an overwhelming presence for years, went about their duties with a different air. Their earpieces still crackled with updates, but their posture had subtly changed. The deference in their manner, while still professional, carried a hint of detachment. They too could sense the shifting winds of power.

The Initial Shock

The "safe" seats he had chosen with such careful calculation were proving to be anything but safe. Numbers flashed across the giant screens—each update worse than the last. The exit polls, which had offered a glimmer of hope despite being less favorable than usual, now seemed like cruel jokes. Reality was far more brutal than even the most pessimistic predictions.

His party office, once the epicenter of power and influence, now stood nearly deserted. Where crowds had once gathered in their thousands, now stood only a handful of party workers. They shuffled awkwardly, avoiding eye contact with the media personnel who had begun to gather like vultures sensing death. The same reporters who had once hung on his every word now barely concealed their smirks as they reported his impending defeat.

The Digital Silence

His phone, usually silent only by choice to avoid disturbance, now lay before him with its volume turned to maximum. The screen remained stubbornly dark. The constant stream of calls from sycophants and favor-seekers had dried up overnight. WhatsApp groups that once buzzed with activity had fallen silent. The digital silence was deafening.

Social media, which his team had managed with such care over the years, was turning hostile. Memes about his defeat were going viral. Videos of his past arrogance were being widely shared. The carefully constructed digital image was crumbling as rapidly as his electoral prospects.

The Unfolding Defeat

The television screens in his office, once his window to his own greatness, now became instruments of torture. News anchors who had praised him just yesterday were now dissecting his failure with barely concealed glee. "A historic defeat," they called it. "The people's verdict against arrogance and corruption." Each analysis felt like a personal attack, each commentary a reminder of his fall.

His assistant's voice trembled as he announced the completion of each round of counting. The numbers were devastating. His opponent, someone he had dismissed as a political lightweight, someone whose calls he had never deigned to answer, was now leading by an unassailable margin. In both constituencies—a double humiliation that would become part of political folklore.

The Family Reality

Even his family had begun to show the strain of impending defeat. His wife's pointed remarks about "what we'll do now" cut deeper than any political analysis. Their children, who had grown accustomed to a life of privilege, watched the proceedings with poorly disguised panic in their eyes. The family that had enjoyed the fruits of power now faced the prospect of a drastically different life.

The servants, sensing the shift in power, had already begun to show subtle signs of insubordination. Requests were met with delays, orders with excuses. The household staff that had once jumped at his every command now moved with deliberate slowness, their actions reflecting the changed reality even before it was officially confirmed.

The Hours of Decline

Hour after hour, the situation worsened. The tick-tick-tick of the wall clock seemed to echo the countdown to his political extinction. He hadn't taken a sip of water since morning, his throat as dry as his political prospects. Several times he caught himself hoping this was just a nightmare, that he would wake up in his ministerial bungalow to find everything normal. But the harsh reality refused to dissolve.

By evening, it was all over. He had lost both seats, and lost them badly. His security deposits, once a mere formality, were forfeited—a final humiliation in a day full of them. The margin of defeat was so huge that even his most loyal supporters couldn't spin it as anything but a complete rejection by the people.

The Empty Corridors

The party office, once his fortress, now felt like a prison. The photographs on the walls—showing him with various dignitaries, cutting ribbons, addressing crowds—seemed to mock him. Each image a reminder of the power he had wielded and lost. The leather chair behind his desk, its armrest still bearing that white towel of privilege, no longer felt like his throne.

The corridors that had once been filled with supplicants seeking favors now echoed with emptiness. The visitors' room, where people had waited hours for a moment of his time, stood deserted. Even the security personnel seemed fewer, their presence already being redirected to more important locations.

The Public Face

He tried to maintain a facade of dignity, attempting to smile for the cameras as he "accepted the people's mandate." But inside, he was screaming. The weight of his new reality crushed down upon him: no more pilot cars, no more sirens clearing his path, no more officials jumping to attention at his arrival. The thought of returning to a normal life seemed impossible—how does one walk after years of being carried?

The press conference was a study in humiliation. Reporters who had once competed for his attention now asked pointed questions about his defeat. The same media that had amplified his every achievement now dissected his every failure. His attempts at maintaining composure only made him appear more pathetic in the eyes of observers.

The Inventory of Loss

The inventory of loss ran through his mind like a bitter litany: the sprawling bungalow he would have to vacate, the fleet of cars that would no longer be at his disposal, the army of assistants and yes-men who would disappear overnight. The privileged life he had come to see as his birthright was slipping away like sand through his fingers.

But worse than the material losses was the death of his power. No more would his phone calls make bureaucrats tremble. No more would his words be treated as commands. No more would people wait for hours just for a moment of his time. He had become what he feared most—ordinary.

The Night of Realization

As night fell, he sat alone in his office, the darkness matching his mood. The phone remained silent, the corridors empty. Through the window, he could see his official vehicles—tomorrow they would be gone. The realization hit him with physical force: he couldn't even cry. The emotions were too deep, too complex for mere tears.

The defeat was total, not just electoral but existential. He had lost not just an election but his entire identity. Who was he without the trappings of power? What was he without the authority of office? These questions haunted him as he sat in the gathering darkness, unable to move forward, unable to go back.

The Final Hours

The clock continued its merciless countdown, each tick marking the passage of time toward his final exit from the corridors of power. Tomorrow, he would have to begin the humiliating process of moving out, of becoming just another face in the crowd. But tonight, he sat frozen in his chair, a deposed king in an empty court, finally understanding—too late—the true cost of power.

Outside, the city continued its normal rhythm, indifferent to his personal tragedy. The same people who had once scrambled for his attention now walked past his office without a second glance. Democracy, that great equalizer, had rendered its verdict. The people he had forgotten while in power had remembered to forget him when it mattered most.